The Kingdom of Colors, Words, and Sounds

The Kingdom of Colors, Words, and Sounds

by

Charles Shelton

ISBN: 978-1-7336235-0-6

DEDICATION

I would like to dedicate this book to my sons Marcus, and Clifton, and to my daughter Leah, to whom, if it weren't for them, I probably would not have become a successful writer.

ACKNOWLEDGMENTS

I would like to give special thanks to my beautiful wife for her love and support.

Besides my wife, I would like to thank our children and grandchildren for their patience and understanding concerning the time and labors needed to bring forth this completed work; but, especially, for the joy and happiness that they bring to us.

In addition, I would also like to thank my brothers and sisters for the encouragement and support that they've provided throughout my life in general.

Lastly, and most of all, thanks be to God for all of the wonders of his creation and the marvelous demonstrations of his love.

INTRODUCTION

There once was a large kingdom in the land of Nog that stood as one. But then it began to unravel, and then it became undone. The reason why is because its subjects or citizens began to quarrel, quibble, and fight amongst themselves. Subsequently, it got so bad, that they decided to split up and live separate from one another. So forming their own kingdoms, the people divided into three separate groups or kingdoms. The names of the new kingdoms were: (1) the Kingdom of Colors, (2) the Kingdom of Words, and (3) the Kingdom of Sounds.

All three kingdoms remained in the huge territory of Nog. However, the Kingdom of Colors moved and took up residence in the northern part of the country. The Kingdom of Words migrated and settled in the east. And, lastly, the Kingdom of Sounds moved to the west. Also, to ensure that they keep separate from one other, the kingdoms built tall walls and fences to keep, quote *"the enemy,"* out.

Interestingly, as respects the people or citizens of the Kingdom of Colors, by nature they are all gifted, visual artists, who create wonderful, colorful works of art on canvases and other materials, using paints, chalks, crayons, and so forth....

beautiful works that stimulate and please the senses; things that captivate the mind, inspire thought, and spread joy and happiness to the heart. Truly, they are all very creative and skilled in what they do. However, on the flipside of things, they happen to be only one dimensional, meaning that they are only capable of doing one thing extremely well, which in their case, is that of working with colors alone.

As regards the citizens of the Kingdom of Words, by nature they are all highly intelligent people, who have very large and extensive vocabularies. They are literary scholars, writers, playwrights, and poets, who love to read and write, and verbalize with eloquent phrases of speech; the kind of words that feed the mind and enlighten the soul, that spread knowledge and wisdom wherever they go. However, just like the people of the Kingdom of Colors, they too are just one dimensional, in that they are good at only one thing alone, and that is with words.

And, last, but not least, in regards to the subjects of the Kingdom of Sounds; they are all inherently talented musicians, who play a variety of musical instruments, and compose a wide genre of songs. The kind of music that delights the ears and brightens the day, that brings joy, excitement, and cheer, from day to day, and from year to year. Yes, they are all highly accomplished musicians, who know their individual instruments well. But, like the people of the Words and the Colors kingdoms, they too are one dimensional only, because this is all that they know how to do well.

~

Eventually, many years pass by — so many years, that the people end up forgetting the initial reason why they split up. All they remember is that they hate each other, and that seems to them to be a good enough reason to always keep far away and separate from the now opposing kingdoms. But, what is even stranger is that as the years pass the people of the three separate kingdoms, for some unexplained and unknown reason, begin to lose the natural abilities they once possessed. Subsequently, their talents begin to gradually diminish, fall flat, and fade away, so that they no longer flow so naturally and easily from them. Because of this, they eventually get frustrated and angry, and in the end they wind up completely giving up on them. Sure, a few people from time to time, struggle every now and then to try to recapture or regain what they had in the past, but without any success.

BAND ON THE RUN

Today, in the Kingdom of Sounds, a young musical band, called "The Mystifires" is performing outdoors before a large, gathered crowd. The names of the five Mystifires band members are: *Gigs*. He is the leader of the band, and the guitarist. And he also happens to play the violin too. Then, there's *Rocky*. He is the bass player. Also, there's *Jazzy*. She is the pianist or electronic keyboard player. And there's *Drummy*. He is the drummer. And, last, but not least, is *Toots*. He is the band's trumpeter, who also plays the saxophone and flute too.

The Mystifires band members are all nineteen years old. They have been together as a musical group for about three years. Currently, at the moment, the song they are performing, which happens to be their first song of the night, is one of their new songs that they have recently composed. However, sad to say, things aren't going so well for them. As a matter of fact, from the very moment that they begin their performance, they start to get heckled and booed by the listening audience, who begin shouting rude things at them, saying: "Boo! You sound awful!" and "You're boring!" and "You guys really suck!"

Strangely, the response that the Mystifires band is getting

from the audience doesn't seem to add up or make sense, because the entire musical group is composed of all skilled musicians, who know their instruments very well. But for some unfathomable reason, which is also very puzzling to them; their songs and concerts are always flat and lifeless, like a heart without a beat, or a body without a pulse. And, just like all other previous performances, today they are quickly booed off stage.

A STRANGE MEETING

Two pairs of beaming eyes lie intently fixed upon one another, staring at each other through a tall, chain-link fence that separates the *Kingdom of Sounds* from the *Kingdom of Words*.

The owners of these curious eyes belong to two young children, who are thoroughly mesmerized, completely captivated by one another. Why? Because neither one of them has ever seen or met anyone who lives on the other side of the fence before.

Totally overcome by their fascination of each other, not a single word is being spoken by either child during this strange and unarranged meeting. Both of them just simply stand there in absolute silence, staring at each other through the all enclosing and restrictive fence. Then, suddenly, out of curiosity, the child from the *Sounds Kingdom* reaches his hand out and he tries to squeeze it through one of the diamond shaped openings in the chain-link fence, in order to touch the child from the *Words Kingdom*. But, before he is able to reach his hand completely through to the other side, the boy is grabbed from behind by his mother, who quickly pulls him back and away from the fence. Next, without missing a beat, the mother takes hold of her son by his ear, and she begins twisting and turning it. In immediate response, the boy, whose name is Fiddler, yells: "Ouch, ouch, ouch, that hurts!"

"Fiddler… what did I tell you? Stay away from those *Words people*!" the Mother says, with a loud, commanding, and scolding voice.

The mother now proceeds to lead the boy by his ear all the way across a grassy field, and into a house that's located in the distance, not too far away. And, as soon as they both enter the residence, the door slams shut behind them, creating a big bang! A loud noise that reverberates and echoes for miles away.

LIGHTS! CAMERA! ACTION!

Today, in the Kingdom of Sounds, the Mystifires band members are all hanging out together. They are over at Gigs house. However, instead of being happy and having a good time, they are bummed out about how their recent attempt to put on a good and successful concert in the local park miserably failed. But also, because of not having anything to do, they are feeling a little sluggish and bored.

"I'm bored," Drummy says, as he sits there with his body slouched down in an oversized chair. Continuing, he says: "We should do something fun and crazy today."

"Like what?" Rocky asks.

"Why don't we sneak over into the *Kingdom of Words* and check it out," Drummy suggests.

"Are you crazy? We can't do that! And even if we did, if we get caught, we'd get in a lot of trouble!" Gigs replies.

"Come on, where's your sense of excitement and adventure?" Drummy inquires.

"Sense of excitement and adventure! It has nothing to do

with excitement and adventure. It's just downright stupid to even think about doing some harebrained, nutty thing like that!" Gigs exclaims.

"I'd be willing to go," Jazzy says.

"You've got to be kidding me, Jazzy! Don't tell me you've lost your mind too?" Gigs remarks, shaking his head back and forth in disbelief.

"Maybe it is crazy? I don't know? I just think it would be fun and exciting to go and check it out; to finally see for ourselves what it's like in the *Words Kingdom*. After all, we are 19 years old and have never seen it. It definitely would be better than just sitting here, moping around and doing nothing at all!" Jazzy declares.

"Let's do it! I'm game!" Toots chimes in and says.

"Okay, but if we get caught, I'm going to put all of the blame totally on you guys," Gigs responds, after finally giving in to the wish and desire of his friends.

Suddenly, a loud voice rings out from another room in the house, saying: "Gigs, don't forget to take the trash out!"

"I will! I was just about to do that, Mom!" Gigs immediately replies to his mother.

~

Later, after having mutually agreed to venture into the *Kingdom of Words*, the Mystifires group swiftly puts together a comprehensive plan on how they intend on getting into the opposing Kingdom. Although, in actuality, it didn't really take much thought at all.

After leaving home the group travels on foot under the

cloak of darkness to the location of a tall, chain link metal fence that boarders and separates the *Kingdom of Words* from the *Kingdom of Sounds*. Once there, they use a large, manual, chain cutter to cut a small opening in the fence—an opening that's large enough for a body to squeeze through. And then, one by one, they proceed to climb through.

Upon stepping foot into the *Kingdom of Words*, the Mystifires quickly enter the city streets, and shortly thereafter they sneak into a brick building called "The Words Playwright Theater." It so happens that the place is so busy and crowded with people that no one seems to notice them slipping in through the front doorway.

After moving towards the back of the theater, the Mystifires proceed to seat themselves in the very back row of seating that resembles wooden bleachers; a location where they feel that they can be both part of the audience, and yet, at the same time remain effectually unnoticed.

~

Today, The Words Playwright Theatre of Actors is putting on a well-known play. It is William Shakespeare's, *Romeo and Juliet*. Delightfully adorned, the actors are all dressed in fanciful clothing worn by people of the Elizabethan era. And, the stage is set up, decorated, and arranged according to the golden age setting of that most distinguished time period.

Romeo now enters onto the stage. And as he approaches Juliet, who stands perched on a balcony of a castle, he says to her: *"But soft, what light through yonder window breaks? It is the east and Juliet is the sun! Arise, fair sun and kill the envious moon, who is already sick and pale with grief, that thou her maid art far more fair than she. Be not her maid since she is envious, her vestal livery is but sick and green, and none but fools do wear it. Cast it off. It is my Lady, O it is my Love…"*

As Romeo speaks, several people in the audience, who quickly become dissatisfied with the seeming lackluster performance of the actor, begin to abruptly and outspokenly voice their complaints, shouting out to him, saying: "Boo… boo!" However, despite this brief and rude interruption by members of the audience, Romeo continues, saying to Juliet, his love: *"The brightness of her cheek would shame those stars, As daylight doth a lamp; her eye in heaven, Would through the airy region stream so bright, That birds would sing and think it were not night…"*

Again, members of the audience boldly interrupt Romeo, yelling: "Boo! You suck!"

As the performance continues, Gigs happens to notice that he and his friends, who are sitting quietly in the back of the theatre, seem to have been spotted by one of the audience members—a highly observant and curious man—who is starting to give them some very strange and suspicious looks.

Juliet now speaks, saying to Romeo: *"O Romeo, Romeo, wherefore art thou Romeo? Deny thy father and refuse thy name. Or if thou will not, be but sworn my love, and I'll no longer be a Capulet… How cam'st thou hither, tell me, and wherefore? The orchard walls are high and hard to climb, and the place death, considering who thou art, if any of my kinsmen find thee here…"*

As Juliet speaks, several people in the audience loudly speak out. And, just like the response that Romeo received, they also begin to heckle her too, saying: "Boo… boo… boring!"

"Wake me when it's over! This play is so lifeless and boring!" one of the audience members complains to a person sitting next to her. She continues, saying: "This humdrum performance is like watching paint dry!"

Once again, Romeo speaks, saying to Juliet: *"With love's light wings did I o'erperch these walls, for stony limits cannot hold love out, and what love can do, that dares love attempt: therefore thy kinsmen are no stop to me…"*

The entire audience now becomes exceedingly restless, vocal, and loud because of the dry, dull, dissatisfying, and lackluster performance of the actors. Consequently, some of them even start to mock Romeo's words. And they shout out mean and humiliating things to him, saying: "Boo! Why don't you take those *'Wings'* and fly away, you frayed feathered chicken!" and "Somebody needs to *'Stop, you,'* because your performance really stinks!" Then, suddenly, the audience begins throwing tomatoes, eggs, and other things at Romeo and Juliet. In response, both Romeo and Juliet quickly and spontaneously put up their guards, and they manage to block the thrown items with shields that they happen to have close at hand. It's almost as though they anticipated or expected this type of reaction from the audience. Afterwards, both of them swiftly and immediately exit the stage.

Now, safely situated backstage and out of harm's way, Juliet (whose offstage name is *Stori*) says to Romeo (whose name is *Telly*), in a sorrowful, irritated, and upset tone of voice: "We did it again, Telly! Although this play was scheduled for continuous shows for the next two weeks, we always get cancelled opening night!"

"You've got that right, Stori! We never even make it through the opening performance without getting booed and rejected!" Telly replies. He continues, saying: "It makes it hard to earn a living! If it wasn't for the free tomatoes, eggs, and other food items thrown by the audience, we'd starve to death!"

~

Telly and Stori are both young actors (about 19 years old) who aspire to become great play-actors someday. However, their acting is far from being great. As a matter of fact, they are downright awful! It's not that they missed any of their lines, because they didn't miss a single word. But, rather, the reason why their acting is weak, pathetic, and boring is because they lack something that brings a performance to life. And, although they realize their miserable failures in this regards, for the mere life of them, they can't seem to figure out or put their finger on what it could possibly be.

~

Following the performance, while the audience is being dismissed, the Mystifires band members manage to slip out the backdoor. However, as they are beginning to walk away from the theater, suddenly, Rocky is grabbed from behind by the man who had spotted them earlier, when they were inside the theatre.

Rocky, completely surprised and taken off guard by the man's actions, is totally shocked and terrified! He doesn't know what to do, especially because the man is so frightfully big and strong! As a matter of fact, he is so large and powerful that it looks like he could easily lift up a full grown ox with his bare hands!

"You're not from around here, are you boy?" the Man says with a deep, resonating, and scary voice, as he reaches out his huge hands and grabs hold of Rocky by the lapels of his upper garment.

"Let me go!" Rocky pleads with the man.

"I'm taking you to the Refereeum! (the local authorities)," the Man says, as he starts to drag Rocky away with him.

"Let him go, you big, ugly, hairy ape!" Drummy yells to the man, in defense of his friend, Rocky. However, the man refuses to listen. He just continues dragging Rocky away with him. Subsequently, Drummy, in an attempt to help his friend, spontaneously and immediately proceeds to run over to and jump on the man's back. However, because the man is so massively large and mighty, he manages to quickly shake him off like a feather. And then, he (the man) also reaches out and grabs hold of Drummy too. Afterwards, he begins carrying both him and Rocky away—one under each of his powerful arms.

"Let us go! Let us go!" the boys frantically and desperately plead with the man. But, with no success.

Suddenly and unexpectedly, out of nowhere, the man is struck on top of his head by a solid and thick wooden club. The blow is so hard that it causes him to instantly release his hold on the boys. And he falls down flat to the ground; knocked out cold!

Standing above the man with a large club in his hand, is Telly, the actor from The Words Playwright Theatre. As it turns out, both he and Stori happened to hear Rocky's and Dummy's cries for help, and they quickly came to their rescue and aid.

"Thanks for your help!" Jazzy happily and thankfully says, as she walks over to and thanks both Telly and Stori for their timely and brave assistance in helping her friends.

"No problem," Telly replies.

"Oh, by the way, my name is Jazzy," Jazzy says, as she reaches out and shakes both Stori's and Telly's hands.

"Hi Jazzy. I'm Telly, and this is Stori," Telly says, as he introduces himself and Stori to Jazzy.

"Where are you guys from, Jazzy?" Stori asks.

"My friends and I are from the *Kingdom of Sounds*," Jazzy

replies.

"We thought so," Telly says. He continues, saying: "Don't you know that you're not supposed to be here?"

"We know," Jazzy responds. "But we were curious, so we thought we'd sneak into your kingdom and check things out for ourselves."

"That's a little crazy and dangerous, don't you think?" Telly responds.

"Yeah, we know. But what's life like without a little excitement and adventure from time to time," Jazzy smiles and says.

"True," Telly agrees. "But now that you have the opportunity and chance, you guys better leave while the going is still good.

So without delay, but not before everybody quickly introduces themselves to one another, the Mystifires leave, and they travel back to the opening in the fence from which they came. And, after reaching the fence, they squeeze their bodies through it, and head for home.

PICTURE THIS

Today, in the Kingdom of Colors, one of the young local artists named, Leonardo Brushshinski, who is 19 years old, is displaying his paintings at a local art exhibit.

During the art show, one of the visitors of the viewing audience proceeds to ask Leonardo a question, concerning one of his paintings, which happens to be a very vivid and colorful work of art, saying: "Young man, what is the title or theme of this painting?"

"Um… um… I guess it doesn't have a title," Leonardo replies with an uncertain and nervous tone of voice.

"What were you trying to capture or say in this painting?" another viewer inquisitively asks Leonardo.

"Um, um… I, I… r-r-really, don't know," Leonardo stutters and says, as he struggles to find the right words to say. In response, the visitors and viewers, now, with lost interest and disappointed looks on their faces, turn and walk away.

"Man… was that uncomfortable!" Leonardo whispers to himself. Continuing, he says: *"Boy… I really suck when it comes to expressing my thoughts and explaining my works of art to others! I don't know why I always freeze up and get so tongue-tied? Something's gotta change, because I haven't sold one of my paintings yet!"* Leonardo disappointingly says to himself.

THE PLAYING FIELD

Today, over in the Kingdom of Sounds, the members of the Mystifires band, along with Telly and Stori from the *Words Kingdom,* with whom the Mystifires have recently become good friends with (ever since they met that special and unforgettable night outside of The Words Playwright Theatre), are out walking together in the outskirts of the *Kingdom of Sounds.* It so happens that they are all secretly headed to an open field in the Sounds Kingdom to play a game of Wickity Stick, although being together is something that is strongly forbidden by the feuding kingdoms, and something that would surely get them in deep trouble if they were to get caught.

∼

"Wickity Stick" is a game that is somewhat similar to baseball, but only it is played with fewer players. Each team consists of just three players (instead of the nine players per team in baseball), which makes Wickity Stick a lot quicker and faster pace than baseball. Also, it has only five innings, instead of nine. And the game has a much bigger stick or club than a baseball bat, and a larger ball too. Also, it has just three bases to run instead of four. In addition, in the game of Wickity Stick there is only one designated pitcher, who is completely neutral, meaning that he or she is not on either of the opposing team's side. It is his or her job to pitch only, and fairly to both teams. Also, batters cannot be struck out. They get to swing at the ball until they make contact, at which time they are then required to run the bases with the intention to score. He or she, who makes it to third base or home without being tagged out in the process, scores. Also, after three players are either tagged out, or three fly balls are caught (or a combination of the two) per inning, then the opposing team's trade sides, meaning that the team that is up to bat goes out into the outfield to play defense, and the team in the outfield goes up to bat. And at the conclusion of the game, after five innings of play are over, the team with the most scores wins the game. However, in the event or case of a tie, then both teams win.

~

"A pap a tee tap, a pap a tee tap, a pap a tee tap, a tap… A pap a tee tap, a pap a tee tap, a pap a tee tap, a tap…" goes the sound of drumsticks beating on a hard object.

"Hey, Drumstir! Can I ask you a question," Telly says to Drummy, as Dummy beats his drumsticks on a fallin tree stump as he passes by, along the long route to the Wickity Stick playing field.

"Sure, Telly. What do you want to know," Drummy replies.

"Why do you always carry your drumsticks everywhere you go, and beat them on everything along the way?" Telly Asks. Continuing, he says: "A pap a tee tap, a pap a tee tap, a pap a tee tap, a tap… That's all I hear coming from you, man!"

"I'm sorry dude, but I can't help it. It's in my blood," Drummy replies.

"No need to apologize. It's perfectly ok. I totally understand. Because, I too, have the same inherited botheration; a self absorbing, innate adoration or infatuation for something that energetically drives my very being, and yet, when satisfied, nourishes the very depths of my soul. Unfortunately, it is a creative itch that needs to be regularly appeased and scratched, so as not to unduly torment the heart and mind. However, in my case, it isn't the need to beat on drums; but rather, it is an insatiable appetite and passion for words, by means of composing scripts, and writing of poems, theatrical plays, and things like that," Telly says.

"You do have a special gift for words, that's for sure!" Drummy replies to Telly.

The group now arrives at the playing field.

The first up to bat is Rocky. And the first time that he swings at the Wickity Stick ball, he hits the ball so hard that he just about knocks the cover off of it! In the process the ball goes flying high up into the sky, and it soars clear over a tall and long, brick wall that separates the *Kingdom of Sounds* from the *Kingdom of Colors,* landing clear on the opposing kingdom's side. Unfortunately, the ball happens to be a special gift that was given to Toots by his father, who was a Wickity Stick legend in his day. And, because of the affixed sentimentality that's rightfully attached to the highly treasured object, Toots becomes highly disappointed and upset over the lost.

"Oh, no! You've got to be kidding me! Come on, Rocky! Why did you have to go and hit the ball over the wall?" Toots disappointedly cries out loud.

"I didn't mean to! It was an accident!" Rocky apologetically replies.

"No it wasn't! You did it on purpose... just to be mean!" Toots shouts.

"I did not! It was an accident!" Rocky repeatedly claims, with a slight grin on his face.

"Well, you better go and get it!" Toots demands. He continues, saying: "Because it's the only ball we've got! But not only that, it was a gift from my father!"

"I'm not gonna fetch it! We're forbidden to go into the *Kingdom of Colors!*" Rocky exclaims.

"That didn't stop you from going into the *Kingdom of Words!*" Toots replies.

"That was different!" Rocky says.

"In what way was it different?" Toots asks.

"We all went together," Rocky says.

"You big wuss!" Toots shouts.

"I'm not a wuss! You're the wuss!" Rocky replies.

"Knock it off, you two!" Stori says to the arguing boys. She continues, saying: "Don't worry, I'll go and get it! Just help me over the wall."

"Hold on, Stori. It's okay. You don't have to go alone. I'll go with you, seeing that it was my fault that the ball wound up over there in the first place," Rocky finally gives in and says.

"No. I can go. I don't mind," Stori replies.

"Okay, but I'll go with you anyways," Rocky says.

"I'll go too," Toots shouts. Afterwards, the three of them immediately approach and begin scaling the wall, with the literal help and support of the rest of their friends.

~

After, Stori, Toots, and Rocky successfully climb over the wall, they happen to immediately spot the Wickity Stick ball. It is lying on the ground, next to the body of a young man, who is lying face down on the ground.

As Stori, Toots, and Rocky slowly approach the lifeless body, Toots, now frightened and worried, imagining that the person is dead (as the result of possibly getting struck in the head by his Wickity Stick ball), turns and he says to Rocky: "Oh no, now look at what you've done! You killed somebody!"

As Toots reaches down to retrieve his Wickity Stick ball, suddenly, the lifeless body moans, and then it moves.

Startled at first, Toots quickly jumps back and away from the body! And then, he turns, and excitedly says to Stori and Rocky: "He's alive!" Afterwards, the three of them approach and help the young man to stand upon his feet.

"Are you okay?" Stori asks the young man.

"I'm alright... I think," the Young Man says, as he rubs his sore head.

Still feeling a little drowsy, disoriented, and dizzy from the blow, the young man asks: "What happened?"

"You got hit by a Wickity Stick ball," Stori says.

"What in the heck is a Wickity Stick ball?" the Young Man asks; being totally unfamiliar with the *Kingdom of Sounds* sport and game.

"Never mind, it's just a ball," Toots says; not wanting to explain in detail.

"All I remember is that I was on my way home from the art exhibit," the Young Man recalls.

"My name is Stori, and this is Toots, and Rocky," Stori says to the young man, as she turns and points to and introduces each of her friends.

"Hello, my name is Leonardo Brushshinski," the Young Man replies, as everyone proceeds to reach out and shake one another's hands.

Interestingly and unexpectedly, from this day forward, Leonardo, along with Stori, Toots, Rocky, and the rest of their associates, without the knowledge and consent of their parents and others (who, if they knew or were ever to find out, would totally and strongly object to the mere thought of it), all become good and close friends.

BAND REHEARSAL

Today, Leonardo, Stori, and Telly have secretively traveled to the Kingdom of Sounds to get together and spend some time with the Mystifires band, which whom they are now good friends with.

During their time together, the Mystifires band begins rehearsing their new song for Leonardo, Stori, and Telly to hear—the one that they played at their recent concert that totally flopped. And, even though they have had ample time to practice it since that time, they are still sounding pretty awful.

Thinking that he can perhaps help the band, Leonardo proceeds to offer some assistance to them. However, Gigs, the band leader, is not open to any help or criticism; especially, coming from someone like Leonardo, whom he feels knows nothing about music. So he says to him: "We've been playing music our entire lives! What do you know about music? After all, you ain't nothin but a stupid painter!"

Jazzy, who has a pretty brassy and outspoken disposition and personality, quickly comes to Leonardo's aid and defense, and she says to Gigs: "Gigs, why don't you shut up, and leave Leonardo alone! He hasn't done anything to hurt anybody! He only meant to help! So I think that we should respectfully listen to what he has to say!"

"Okay. You're right. I guess I shouldn't be so quick to judge and condemn," Gigs says to Jazzy.

Next, apologizing to Leonardo, Gigs says: "I'm sorry Leonardo, man."

"That's okay," Leonardo humbly replies to Gigs.

"So what were you thinking?" Gigs, asks Leonardo.

"Well... and please don't take this the wrong way. But, for one, you guys need to learn to play together and feed off of each other. Now, I know that you are all very skilled musicians. But you have the tendencies to try to outshine, outdo, or outplay each other. Don't do that. Don't show off! Learn to exercise some restraint, and just play beautiful music. Also, Drummy, you're playing way too loud, man! So tone it down a bit, will ya! Your goal should be to complement your fellow musicians, not to drown them out! And last, and most of all, all of you need to learn to play with *Colorful* feelings and emotions, which will help to bring your music to life, and give your individual songs their own voice or distinct character. Right now, all of the different songs that you play sound the same, because they are emotionless or colorless. In other words, they lack real feeling and soul! You see, 'colors to sounds' are like 'spices are to food.' For one, they give it flavor and make it taste really good. So let's try the song again from the top, but this time, try to put some *Color* in it!"

"Okay, we'll try," the Band Members say. Afterwards, they gear themselves up to replay their song.

Unfortunately, as soon as the band begins to replay their song, the door to where they are located is forcefully broken open, and the Refereeum, who are the local police authorities, grab and arrest Telly, Stori, and Leonardo.

Totally blown away by the unbelievable and upsetting scene that is unfolding before their eyes, and not knowing what to say or do, the Mystifires band members remain silent, as they just stand there completely shocked and dumfounded, watching their friends being unjustly apprehended and arrested, like they are hardened criminals or something.

"You are hereby under arrest for unauthorized entry into the Kingdom of Sounds!" the head Refereeum says to Telly, Stori, and Leonardo. And then, continuing, he says: "And you are to be immediately taken into custody, where you will remain until you stand trial!" Afterwards, he and his accompanying strongmen quickly whisk the three young people away.

ORDER IN THE COURT

Today, Telly, Stori, and Leonardo are being tried by the official "High Court of Appeals" of the *Kingdom of Sounds*. On hand to witness the hearing are Telly, Stori, and Leonardo's parents, and also the Mystifires band members, as well as the high governing officials of both the *Kingdom of Words* and the *Kingdom of Colors*, along with many of its prestigious and concerned citizens.

"What is the penalty for unauthorized entry into the *Kingdom of Sounds*?" The presiding Magistrate or Judge asks his court officials.

"Life in prison, Your Honor," the head Prosecutor says. He continues, saying: "It is a relevant or pertinent law that was established by our most distinguished and illustrious forefathers of the past, concerning a matter such as this—a law that has been passed down for decades."

"Who is representing these young people who are being tried today?" the Judge asks.

"I guess, I am, seeing that you don't allow outsiders to participate," Telly answers.

"Alright then," the Judge replies.

Approaching Telly the Prosecutor says to him: "How dare you young people openly defy authority and step into the forbidden *Kingdom of Sounds!* Who gave you permission to do so?"

"No one, Sir," Telly replies.

"Then, why would you do such a thing?" the Prosecutor

asks.

"I don't know. I guess we were just curious, Sir," Telly responds.

"Haven't you ever heard the expression 'Curiosity killed the cat?'" the Prosecutor asks.

"Yes, I'm totally familiar with that saying, Sir," Telly replies. And then, continuing, he says: "However, and I say this with all due respect. It doesn't seem just and practical to deny people the right to choose for themselves whom they wish to have as associates and friends. After all, we didn't do anything wrong. We were just spending and having a good time with our newly formed friends from the *Kingdom of Sounds*."

"I beg to differ on that opinion young man! Because you're too young to know what's right and good for you! Therefore, it is our job as adults and leaders of the people to decide that for you. It's for your own protection and good, no matter how you prefer to see it!" the Prosecutor says.

"In all due respect, Sir, I'd have to say that the choices that you, the 'Kingdom Rulers,' and other person's of authority initially made in the past, in regards to both having and keeping the three kingdoms separate from each other, have been, to a large degree, very undermining and crippling to all of us over the years, including yourselves," Telly exclaims.

"Undermining and crippling? Ha! My word, dear son! Have you simply lost your mind? What in the world could you inferior people ever be able to do or offer to us that could possibly help us in any fashion, form, or way? After all, we don't need you, or anyone else for that matter! Because, as distinct, beautiful, and great individuals, we the people of the *Kingdom of Sounds* are complete in all respects within ourselves," the

Prosecutor remarks.

"I'm sure that as a people, you are very competent, self sustaining, and highly proficient in many respects, Sir. However, when it comes to some things in life, it can be extremely helpful and beneficial to get the perspective or viewpoint of an outsider; from someone who sees things a little differently than we ourselves might. However, sad to say, from the way things are sounding and looking here today; unfortunately, I don't think that there is anything that I can verbally say that will convince or sway you to think otherwise. But perhaps, there is something else that can," Telly says.

Jazzy, now speaks up, and she says to the court in behalf of her friends on trial: "Excuse me, Your Honor, Sir. My name is Jazzy. And I'd like to tell you that Stori, Telly, and Leonardo are really good people, who are dear, close, and wonderful friends of ours; friends that have taught us a lot about ourselves; who have helped us in so many ways! But not only that, we are so much better, stronger, and happier now when we are with them!"

"That's very hard for me to both imagine and believe, little Lady," the Prosecutor says.

"Allow us to show you, Your Honor," Gigs speaks up and says to the Judge.

The Judge thinks about it for a moment, and then he says: "Okay, then proceed. We'll give you just one chance to prove your point."

The Mystifircs band now sets up their band instruments, which they brought along with them, and they begin to play. However, as hard as they try, their music still sucks! And, immediately, they are booed by the listening crowd. So the band becomes disheartened and they stop playing.

"Man, do we suck!" Drummy says to his fellow band members in a highly disappointed tone.

"Gigs, remember what I told you!" Leonardo yells out from the confines of his seat. He continues, saying: "Play together, with *Colorful* emotions and feelings!"

After hearing what Leonardo says, Gigs looks over at the Judge, and he says to him: "Your Honor, can we have one more chance?"

"You may," the Judge says.

Gigs, now turns, and he speaks to everyone present in the courtroom, and he says: "This is a new song that me and the band have been working on. It's called 'I Am You, and You Are Me.'"

The band now quickly regroups, and then they begin playing again.

As the band members begin to play, they wholeheartedly apply Leonardo's advice, which has immediate and unbelievable, good results. Totally shocked and amazed within themselves by the vast improvement to their sound and song, the band members faces light up and glow with happy and satisfied big smiles. But, not only this, Telly and Stori also join in, by spontaneously adding words or lyrics to the song, as they lend their voices and sing along. As a result, their appropriate and wonderful lyrics add even more depth and life to the music, and gives special meaning and feelings to the already amazing sound!

When the crowd hears the band playing in a way that they

have never heard before, and Stori and Telly singing along, they are completely blown away by the amazing, exciting, and heart-stirring sound! Many of them are even moved to tears! The sound of the instruments playing is absolutely inspiring, charming, and delightful. And the singing voices are like the voices of angels. Just listen to the words of the song:

I am you, and you are me,
Together we make each other complete
You've got your strengths, and I've got mine,
We fit together like rhythm and rhyme
You are the heart, and I am the beat,
Life with you is ever so sweet
So take my hand and let's walk as one,
Into the rays of the rising sun

(Chorus)
I am you, and you are me,
Together we make each other complete
Blessed are we,
Yes blessed we are
Joyful are we,
Yes happy we are

Once we were lost, but now we're found,
Cause we learned to live on common ground
You've got your strengths, and I've got mine,
When we put 'um together, a real treasure we find
You are the color, and I am the sound,
Together we make the music go round
You are the lyrics, and I am the voice,
So bring on the music, let's dance and rejoice

(Chorus)
I am you, and you are me,
Together we make each other complete

Blessed are we,
Yes blessed we are
Joyful are we,
Yes happy we are

I am you, and you are me,
And together we make each other complete.

~

Immediately, after the song is finished playing, the entire room is move to tears, and the people all burst out in loud applause and cheers! For they have never heard anything as lovely and beautiful as this in all their years!

Interestingly, as respects the Mystifires band, by themselves they are not much. But when you put or mix their *Sounds* together with beautiful *Colors* and *Words,* then they become magnificently stupendous! The same is true in regards to all other aspects of the people lives in general within the three divided kingdoms. Living and keeping separate from one another makes them weaker and incomplete, but when they all come together and harmoniously combine as one united group, and freely share their innate abilities and gifts with one another, and feed off of each other, then it makes them a whole lot better, fuller, and complete, which in turn, enriches, and adds to their overall enjoyment, success, and happiness in life.

THE SOUND OF MUSIC

Today, in the large Kingdom of Nog, the Mystifires band is performing outdoors before a large, gathered crowd. As it so happens, there in attendance, are people from the Sounds, Words, and Colors Kingdoms. For the people are no longer divided by ugly, destructive, and inhibiting fences and walls. But rather, the three separate kingdoms have (because of the beauty, happiness, and success of the Mystifires band and their new found friends from the Colors and Words kingdoms) decided to reunite, and once again form one solid and united kingdom, that now happens to be a whole lot better and happier than the previous one that existed in the past.

Interestingly, as the Mystifires are performing they are not getting booed. But instead, they are receiving big cheers, applause, and standing ovations from the mixed crowd of highly satisfied people. As a matter of fact, their performance is completely blowing the audience away! The reason why is because their band and music are so much better now, because they play with exciting and moving *Colors,* and they have inspiring and beautiful *Words* in their songs.

HARK, I HEAR A VOICE

Today, in the Kingdom of Nog, The Words Playwright Theatre of Actors is putting on a well-known play. It is William Shakespeare's, *Romeo and Juliet.*

Romeo now speaks to Juliet, his love, as she stands perched on a balcony of a castle, he says to her: *"But soft, what light through yonder window breaks? It is the east and Juliet is the sun! Arise, fair sun and kill the envious moon, who is already sick and pale with grief, that thou her maid art far more fair than she. Be not her maid since she is envious, her vestal livery is but sick and green, and none but fools do wear it. Cast it off. It is my Lady, O it is my Love…"*

Juliet says to Romeo: *"O Romeo, Romeo, wherefore art thou Romeo?…"*

"Bravo! Bravo!" the listening audience shouts.

Why are Stori and Telly's performance so much better and appreciated now, than they were in the past? The reason why is because now they have infused *Colors* — stirring emotions and passion into their speech and performance. And their plays are accompanied by beautiful orchestrated *Sounds*. As a matter of fact, Stori's and Telly's performance is so compelling and good that it brings the women in the audience to tears! Even some of the men are a little choked up, with tears running down their beards!

In the end, *Romeo and Juliet* become a sensational smash hit with audiences throughout the kingdom. It is so successful that it goes on to get booked to sold-out audiences for the next six months!

A BEAUTIFUL WORK OF ART

Today, in the Kingdom of Nog, an art exhibit is on display. One of the young local artists named, Leonardo Brushshinski, is displaying his paintings, with the soft sounds of a flute playing in the background. It is his friend Toots, playing joyful songs on his flute.

During the art show, one of the visitors of the viewing audience proceeds to ask Leonardo a question, concerning one of his paintings, which happens to be a very vivid and colorful work of art, saying: "Young man, what is the title or theme of this painting?"

"I call this piece 'Dancing Leaves!'" Leonardo immediately says.

"Ah, that's a very interesting, appropriate, and intriguing title," the person admirably says with a big and glowing smile on their face.

"Your painting is simply delightful, absolutely magnificent!" another member of the viewing audience remarks. And then, continuing, she says: "It is the most beautiful work of art I have ever seen! I don't know what price you're asking for it, but, whatever it is, I'll take it!"

"Thank you," Leonardo responds with an extremely happy countenance and voice.

Interestingly, by the end of the day, as it turns out, not only did Leonardo sell this painting, but he sold everything that he had on display!

Why is it that Leonardo's art showings are so much better and successful now, than they were in the past? The reason why is because he now has *Words* to help express the true meaning of his art. And his art exhibits are supported by lovely musical *Sounds*.

HAPPILY THEREAFTER

As days, months, and years pass by, the Kingdom of Nog is growing stronger, happier, and more successful day by day. Because all of its citizens have finally figured out what it was that they were missing and lacking, which is the help, assistance, support, and encouragement that they receive from one another. They also learned the valuable lesson that even though people may be different from themselves, that everyone and everything has a special place and purpose in life. And that they should not take one another for granted. For each of them possess special abilities, gifts, and talents that help to make one another better. Without each other they are weaker and incomplete. But when they feed off of each other, help, and encourage one another, they bring out the very best in each other, thereby becoming more effective, powerful, happy, and successful. Sure, they can choose to live separate and without one another, but it will greatly diminish their quality and enjoyment of life. Because *together* we make the world a more enjoyable and beautiful place, by far!

NOTE TO READER